LOST IN THE DESERT

by

Robbie Moffat

PALM TREE PUBLISHING

PALM TREE PUBLISHING
Paisley, Scotland Pa1 1TJ

© Robbie Moffat 1976-2019

First published in digital form JUNE 2014
First published in paperback JANUARY 2019

Typeset: Verdana 11pt

ISBN-10: 0 907282 49 0
ISBN-13: 9780907282495

INTRODUCTION

The story that follows is set in a remote part of Africa. The circumstances that led up to the events, (set on the fringes of the Southern Sahara close to the conjunction of the Sudan, Kenya and Uganda), are related to the outbreak of the Green Monkey disease that swept Juba in October 1976. This killer virus was later redefined as the first ever recorded outbreak of Ebola.

At the time, Sudan was still recovering from its seventeen year civil war. Uganda was under the dictatorship of Idi Amin. The area had been inaccessible for six months due to the rains.

DEDICATION

This book is dedicated to Nigel Silcock and Manari Yoshiro who I never saw again.

> From Khartoum up to Kathmandu,
> from Kabul to Kinshasa -
> everyone is blowing grass.
> everyone is wrecked on hash,
> everyone's completely smash
> on ganja, bang, and charis.

MONDAY

Nightfall came. They sneaked out of the bungalow, first Nigel, then Manari, then James. They hurried across open space to the Kenya Road. None noticed their shadows flirting in the faint light of the new moon.

Setting up a stiff pace, they walked the first mile apprehensive.

Would they be seen?

But there was nothing, only the silence of the sleeping town left behind, and the silence of the unknown ahead. Before them was nothing but black, continuous miles of picking their way along a stone strewn road, each of them wary of twisting an ankle or falling into a pot-hole.

Suddenly ahead, a light danced, stopping them in their tracks.

"Listen!" James hissed. They heard the sound of voices. "Quick! Get off the road."

Half stumbling, they penetrated the undergrowth by the side of the road, thorns pricking at their legs and arms. The light drew nearer. In the twilight of the setting moon, they saw a soldier carrying a torch. He led a small army patrol.

Aroused by the sound of their headlong charge into the bush, the soldier shone his torch in their direction. He caught sight of Manari in the arc of the beam. He un-slung his rifle, pulled back the bolt, and shouted an order in Arabic.

"Ah shit!" James mumbled to Nigel.

All three returned to the road and greeted the soldiers.

"Salem."

James shook the platoon corporal's hand and immediately started clacking away in Arabic.

"Went into the bush for a piss, you know. Nice evening, eh? Well, we're on our way to Kenya, and I suppose we better be pushing on. It's a long way, you know."

The platoon leader hesitated. He turned to the other three soldiers who were busy restraining the herd of goats they were taking into the town. James sensed the soldiers' indecision. He took his chance.

"Good night" he said.

He started swiftly off into the dark with Nigel and Manari close behind. The Sudanese soldiers, bewildered at meeting three foreigners so far in the bush, shrugged their shoulders. Who were they to question three strangers? All they wanted to do was to return to their village and go to sleep.

James, Nigel and Manari walked on for hours and hours, yet by the time they stopped to share a cigarette, they had only covered four miles. They were in bad shape. They had been cooped up for five weeks. James and Nigel had been living on lentils, onions, tomatoes, and squash since they had got on the paddle-steamer at Kosti. They had no idea what Manari had been living on before they met him in Juba. Not that it mattered now. The wilderness eased the pain of their last month. The stars above twinkled on and off between the racing clouds. The trees and dry burnt bush closed in all about. The lonely call of some desert bird made the evening vibrate on every note of melancholic sound.

It was peaceful.

They wanted to stop and spend the night there, but it was just not possible. They had to put as many miles between themselves and the town before the police discovered their escape.

Weary, they carried on and passed through a sleeping village. James' heart shot through his chest as a blood-curdling scream lashed out of the darkness. It terrified his whole being.

It was a hyena.

"I've almost had it with this

continent!"

His nerves were frayed.

Eventually, they dropped their bags and fell asleep by the roadside. For James, it was a night of tossing and turning, fears of killer tribesmen lurking in every dream. Nightmares of miles walked and miles still to be walked. The chance of police pursuit, or of robbers stealing their bags beneath their tired heads, or the threat of torrential rain making deep slumber a sodden misery.

James was full of fear. He and his two companions were running from death.

TUESDAY

Dawn was a toffee for breakfast, a couple of drags on a shared cigarette, a brushing of hair, a tucking-in of shirts, a packing of bags. Then the effort of putting cramped but still un-blistered feet onto the road again.

The road was petering out into a track when they met a semi-naked tribesman; spear in hand, going towards the town.

"Kenya! Kenya! Is it this way?" Nigel asked the tribesman, pointing along the track.

The tribesman nodded his head and gave a big grin. He was a reassuring figure in a growing, uncertain world.

They said their goodbyes and walked on.

The sun in deep red glow appeared from its bed behind the mountains. They saw it's streaks of weak but warming light strike the roofs of a straw-hut village and fall at the feet of a dozen half-awakened men.

Hesitant, the three ambled their way warily towards them.

The men were dressed in army green, here and there a rifle propped against a wall or resting against a leg. Their eyes began to focus and set a careful watch on the strangers approaching. One man shouted and other men appeared from the huts, all caught unawares and a little taken aback at the arrival of the foreigners.

Where was the sentry?

Women peeped from the doorways as the early morning cry of an unfed baby welcomed the three into the village. Hens scurried out of the way of the corporal, who quickly threw some water over his face, tightened his belt, and slung his rifle to his shoulder.

James spotted the corporal advancing on them and extended a friendly hand to dispel any fears.

The corporal shook James's hand briefly while the other men advanced to shake hands in turn. Here and there was a strong one, or one who wasn't sure of his own strength, or one who tried to show he was a rough-tough army man.

James asked the corporal if they could fill their five-litre water container from the village well. The corporal was obliging, but he soon began to ask questions.

The three, trying to ignore his questions, quenched their growing thirst with some cold water from the well.

The corporal asked them where they were going and when they had left Kappoeta, which was now twelve miles behind them. James smiled and waffled and evaded the questions as best he could, while the corporal asked further questions. Finally, the corporal asked if they had permission to be so far into the bush, and could he see their passports.

"Shit" James thought "This guy's looking for too many answers."

James spoke quickly with Nigel and Manari. It was decided that James would show the corporal his passport if it would pacify him. It was a risky business. There was a good chance he would not return it.

"Then what?" Nigel asked.

James took the risk.

The corporal studied the passport, then apparently satisfied, handed it back to James. James wondered if the corporal understood the situation any better.

Yet, from the expression on his face, the corporal was still uncertain about the presence of three foreigners so far into the bush. However, when James asked him which direction they should go in to reach Kenya, he had no reason to be false in his advice.

He took them to the edge of the village and showed them the track to follow. Without looking back, the three set off, leaving the corporal to wonder why they should be heading off into the bush without an escort or guide. Everyone knew how dangerous the road could be.

But was it the corporal's problem? After all, it was not his responsibility to give or let people have permission to travel the road beyond the last military outpost. That sort of permission was given by the command of the town. It was not a decision he had to make. If he shouldn't have let them go, at least he had checked that their passports were in order. What else could he do?

James, Nigel and Manari descended a hill and crossed a large dry riverbed that marked the beginning of no-man's land and the desert. Manari levelled his compass and took a bearing.

A concerned look came over his face. They were heading north-east instead of south.

James insisted the road would swing south soon. Manari disagreed.

Nigel stood by watching.

The sky opened up, and poured its heart out in a sudden cloudburst. It was an omen. Nigel interpreted the sign.

"Cool it" he stated.

James and Manari patched up their differences. The cloudburst soothed the heat. It was the first and last difference of opinion they would have. It was the first and last rainfall they would see in the desert.

Thankful of cloud cover, they walked on into the barren, uninhabitable waste. James and Nigel strode ahead of little Manari. The little Japanese man did not look well. He had a nosebleed.

James and Nigel joked about their companion. Being only five foot-two was a disadvantage for their Japanese friend, a hereditary disadvantage.

"Short legs, short arms, short-sighted" James laughed. "Being a six-foot three European has its disadvantages, though."

"Long arms, long neck and half-mast trousers" Nigel suggested. Nigel was only five foot eleven.

"Cold feet in bed, dry knees in baths, head knocks in doorways, bumped senseless" James replied.

Nigel and James walked ahead for a couple of miles, then gladly rested. They waited for a steady-paced Manari to catch them up. At first they were apprehensive about leaving him half a mile behind. They had heard gruesome stories about the wild tribesmen and killer robbers who inhabited the desert.

"I think the tales of boiled man's head and human heart and liver fry-ups are a bit far-fetched" said Nigel.

It was hard to say. Ever since the tribesmen had raided the town, and the police and the military had retaliated by slaughtering every Taposa tribesmen they could find, an atmosphere of uneasiness had descended on the entire area. The Taposa, a wild tribe of pastoral nomads, had become a self-implanted fear in the minds of the nominally more civilised people of Kappoeta and the outlying villages.

For the Taposa, the citizens of Kappoeta had become hated foes. It was well understood by both sides that there was no case for mercy.

By stopping frequently to check that Manari hadn't disappeared, James and Nigel's confidences grew. Their apprehensions about coming face to face with wild tribesmen lessened. Though the gap between them and Manari widened, there was never more than ten minutes separating them.

The area seemed safe.

They walked for three hours without seeing any sign of human life. The fear of wild animals was a minimal concern during day-light hours. The heat of the sun was much worse than any danger from beast or creature.

Once again, they rested until Manari caught up.

"Cigaretti?" Manari asked. It was one of Manari's few words that his travelling companions could understand.

They lit a cigarette and shared it in turn.

"I wonder when we're going to come upon a water hole?" Nigel asked.

"Don't know, Nig."

During their time under house arrest in Kappoeta, they had heard that there were numerous water holes between the town and the Kenyan village of Lokichogio. They had hoped to reach Lokichogio by nightfall of the following day.

Suddenly, their conversation stalled. A herd of goats scurried out of the bush and on to the track. A young naked boy followed them with a branch in his hand that he employed as a switch to keep his herd in check.

The boy stopped. He rubbed his eyes, and then stood motionless.

James shouted to him in Arabic, requesting water. But the boy, confused at having stumbled upon them so unexpectedly, kept his distance. He appeared to have not understood a word of what James had said.

James rose. Shooing the goats away, he approached the paralysed boy and took hold of his hand.

The boy still remained motionless.

James shook his hand then pointed to his five-litre water container, but the boy just shook his head as if to say he didn't understand. To alleviate his fear, for he was obviously frightened by James, the boy laughed nervously.

James laughed too.

Deciding that trying to communicate was hopeless, and knowing that further words were a waste, James left the boy and returned to the others sitting under a tree. The boy seizing his chance quickly chased his goats back into the bush.

As they talked about the boy, a big strong heavy breasted, very pregnant native woman, her jewelry jingling to the swinging of her breasts, came down the road. On her head, balanced precariously, was a bale of straw that rocked too and fro with her ungainly walk. On seeing the threesome, she pretended they were a figment of her imagination. Deep down she was frightened, not out of fear, but out of ignorance. It was the last place in the world she would expect to see three people of the likes of them. She knew what they were. White men. She had heard others tell stories of them to her, from the frightening to the foolish. Once or twice in the past she had gotten the opportunity to see a white man in her years of trading in the villages on the fringe of the desert. They were aggressive people not to be tampered with. So she kept her distance. She passed by warily with long slow uneasy backward looks.

This made James, Nigel, and Manari uneasy too.

The rest was over.

On their feet again, the sun was climbing higher to make walking a discomfort. Labouring in the heat, Nigel's sweat filled eyes settled on some adobe huts concealed by the barbed desert scrub. He pointed to the huts for the benefit of the others.

The discovery of the settlement threw them into a great indecision. Should they approach the huts? Or not?

Fear had gotten hold of them.

"Hell! This is ridiculous" James exclaimed. "There are three of us. We'll be okay."

They left the road and made their way through the undergrowth. All was quiet. They reached a ring of metre high intertwined thorn branches surrounding the small six hut settlement. Squatting in the enclosure were three semi-naked women, one grinding seed between two stones, another scraping cattle dung out to dry as fuel, the third cleaning pots with sand. These three women were figures from a long lost age.

Nigel threw some pebbles into the compound and drew one of the women's attentions. She immediately froze. The other two women stopped their chores and assessed the strangers. Nigel, with a casual wave and a smile, asked the women in Arabic for water.

"Water?" one of the women said. "Water?" She pointed back down the road. "Try that way! We can't give you any! Go find it yourself."

They accepted the women's general attitude. James thought it typical for the area. No-one had anything to give, so they gave nothing.

They were becoming exceedingly thirsty.

They picked their way back to the road, and trucked on. Half a mile further down the way, they came upon a larger settlement.

"Heh! Old man!" James shouted. "Do you have any water?"

"Piss off! I can't help you. Go find your own" the man gestured.

"Jesus! What a bunch of bastards"

Nigel exclaimed out loud.

"Understandable" James said. "In the desert no-one gives water away when it has the value of gold."

They took the hint and left the old man to his curses. Unexpectedly, they came face to face with two young, naked females, oozing in youthful laughter.

James was struck by their beauty, their naked beauty. In any other situation he would have been attracted to them. Not today. It was too hot. He only had a mind to ask them for water.

The girls, eager to help, pointed in the direction of the road. They communicated with sign language. Arabic was no longer a common language by which to exchange information.

"Water" the girls indicated. "Plenty that way."

They followed the girl's instructions and reached a dried-up riverbed. The road crossed the riverbed, but it had been washed away to a depth of nine feet.

"I don't see any water hole" said Nigel.

"How about a rest?" James asked. "What do you think?"

"Alright" said Nigel.

"O.K!" their little Japanese friend

panted. His nose was still bleeding.

They settled down under the shading branches of a leafless thorn tree, sheltering from the fierceness of the midday sun.   Nigel and Manari spread their sleeping rolls on the sandy ground by the wadi. James's, roll had long since gone. Penniless, he had sold it to a policeman in Kappoeta to finance their journey across the desert.   With the little gain that this had brought in, he had managed to purchase a packet of ten cigarettes, two boxes of matches, a kilo of lentils, three onions, a half kilo of flour, a quarter of tea, four lemons and twenty four butter milk toffees for quick energy release.   For twenty-five English pounds worth of sleeping roll, it was poor exchange.

But James's soul had been worth even less while he had been detained in Kappoeta. How he'd ever managed to get caught up in the whole chain of events, he'd never know.

Already, the major worry was their lack of water.

James made a half survey of the riverbed for a water hole. Something caught his eye. He spun around to see a fifteen-sixteen year old boy carrying a club emerging from the bush. All he wore was a small brown cloak.

The boy strode boldly across the

sandy riverbed towards them. James, Nigel and Manari fell silent and expectant. The boy approached and quickly shook hands with each of them in turn. He was very relaxed, almost too relaxed to be surprised at encountering the threesome. James guessed that the boy had been watching them for a considerable time before emerging from the undergrowth.

The boy did not speak Arabic, but James got it across to him that they were searching for water. The boy in comprehension, pointed along the riverbed, and then curved his hand, to indicate that the water hole was around a bend. James got it across that he wanted the boy to show him, but the boy smiled and lay down upon the sand in the shade of the thorn bush.

Patient, yet bewildered, the travelers did the same. What else could they do? The boy knew where to find water. They had to play along with him.

Time dragged past slowly as they sat waiting. The boy sang to himself. Every now and then, James caught his eye glancing at their belongings. He was curious to see what they possessed.

"Well, I'm getting hungry" Nigel protested. "But I suppose we better be sure of finding more water before we use what's left for cooking and making tea."

"C'mon, kid, give us a break." James said.

The boy just smiled.

Nigel was growing impatient.   He jumped to his feet.

"I'm off to look for water."

The boy jolted by Nigel's action, suddenly sprung to his feet and ran after him.   Both disappeared round the bend.

Five minutes later, the boy came racing back. He was now completely naked. He grabbed Manari's cup, and ran off again to vanish beyond the bend.   James and Manari were tense, and obsessed with the thought that the tribesmen may have ambushed Nigel. For ten minutes they nervously awaited Nigel's return.

"Ah! They come!" Manari shouted in Japanese, delighted at seeing Nigel appear with the water container slung over his shoulder. He had a big smile on his face that beamed warmer than the sun.   The boy accompanied him, the cup in his hand full of clean sparkling water.

"We had to dig a few feet down into the sand to find water" Nigel explained.

"Movie stuff" James replied with a

smile. "Hardly surprising though, seeing it's the start of the dry season."

"I'm hungry" Nigel reiterated.

"Manari, get a fire going, let's have a cup of tea. Squirt one of those lemons in."

Manari set to with the fire that took all of a minute to build and light. The whole bush was a tinderbox. James cut up some onions and washed some lentils. The tea was ready in a jiffy.

"Long live the Tsar!" James toasted. The boy sipped on some tea.

"The kid doesn't like it much without sugar" said Nigel.

"Okay, okay, no need to screw your face up." James scolded the boy humorously. "Here, we've boiled some lentils. Look! With an onion thrown in. That's right … take a piece of bread. We made it before we left the town. Nice, eh. I knew you'd like the lentils. Gee, you must be hungry to scrape out the pot like that."

They had another pot of tea to follow on, then for dessert, a cigarette. With only six left, each one was increasing in value. They passed it round, the boy drawing deep as if he were a Rasta smoking ganja. The cigarette went around twice before the smell of burning filter paper made them stub it out. As they lay down and let the heat of midday pass them by, the boy, a restless creature, touched, felt, and pulled at their possessions, asking, wanting, needing everything they had for himself.

"No! Hands off" James warned him smacking his hand. But the boy was persistent. He wanted James's straw hat, Nigel's tee shirt and socks, Manari's knife. In fact, anything he saw.

James patiently tried to explain to him that the rules of hospitality were such that they should not be abused. "We've given you food, drink and smoke, yet still you're not happy. You showed us water, but we've fed you. You'll have no more."

The boy quietened down and thought awhile. James could see it all in the boy's eyes. I'll show them. Huh! Me Taposa and this Taposa country. Taposa here kill other men. You three white men not safe here. The way is long and alive with Taposa. Now, I am Taposa and can talk to other Taposa while you can say nothing. If you listen to me, you will be safe. I will be your guide; I will lead you through Taposa land. But if you leave without me, I will tell the Taposa to kill you. So do not refuse me. I have power over your lives.

James looked the boy straight in the eye. All the boy's gesturing had cast doubts. Maybe he was bluffing. Then again, what was the point of putting their lives at risk for the sake of a few possessions? All the boy wanted was something from them. He was just trying a little childish blackmail to scare them into giving him anything he wanted.

"He's in a position to make trouble." Nigel said to James.

"Yet why should we be wangled out of our belongings?"

"If we give him a little we might stay out of trouble."

"Alright. Give him something" James said with a shrug.

"Okay, here goes."

Nigel fished out an old pair of nylon socks, a few holes showing here and there. He handed them to James, who held them in front of the boy. The boy's eyes lit up as he reached out for them. James drew them away.

"First things first. You and me are going to fetch some more water. Seeing the locals around here are unfriendly, you can be my guard. How's that. Afterwards, when we get back, you can have the socks. Okay?"

James straightened up, grabbed the water bottle, and threw the socks to

Nigel. The boy, hesitant, made to follow James, then remembered he'd forgotten his club. Picking it up, he chased James, then led the way along the riverbed to the water-hole.

When James and the boy rounded the bend, a few wild sheep were watering at the hole. They soon chased them off.

The air was still.

Tense with expectancy. James kept watch, while the boy seemed a little nervous at James hovering over him. Perhaps he thought that James was going to jump upon him, but James smiled in reassurance to ease the strain.

"The bottle's full, honky" he appeared to say, holding the container up.

"Great!" James replied. "Let's get back to the others."

When they returned, Nigel gave the boy his socks, a pair of brown ankle lengths with green stripes. Totally tasteless. But the boy was elated. An Oxbridge civil servant would have been aghast at seeing a pair of those on the London Underground.

"Rather small, old boy, but they'll stretch in water." James said to the boy as he struggled to put them on his large feet.

The boy gazed at the pair of socks James was wearing and then pointed out that the pair he had been given only came up to his ankles. James's socks went beyond his calves. James dismissed his observations with a smile, thumbs up sign, and a slap on the boy's back.

"No more complaints, okay? Good."

One more cup of tea later, they packed up and set out on the road again.

They were becoming aware of the pitfalls of the road.

Sometimes insatiable dreams of hidden paradises keep the spirit moving right up to the end. Then something goes snap! It's like hot air escaping from a balloon floating over arêtes and snow covered peaks. A rapid plummet, a last reflection on the beauty of being on top looking downwards, before everything rushes up. And bang!

The boy led the way, club in his right hand, socks in his left. He set a good pace for two, three miles, until eventually he dropped further and further behind. At last, he disappeared altogether, swallowed up by the bush. Once more, the threesome were on their own, as the sun began to set, assaggied to death as Zulu legend has it, by the one-limbed, one-eyed spearman.

As sunset came, James's chief concern was the nagging blisters on his feet. He had begun to limp.

"That damned ditch" he cursed. It had been pitch dark and he had fallen into a road ditch one evening back in the town. His left knee was still weak. A large puffy blister between the ball and toes of his left foot caused him to turn his ankle inwards. This put further strain on his out-turned knee.

"Shit!" was all that Nigel heard James say.

Manari, meanwhile, had worn holes through his socks, and Nigel's tennis shoes were about to split. The broken rock on the road made for tedious walking. But they managed to raise their heads to watch the graceful exit of the sun. In the distance, a range of hills poked their jagged summits up out of the lifeless bush. The gentle breeze, caught in their sun-bleached hair momentarily tinted orange by the last arching rays of the sun setting in the west.

Their thoughts became scattered on a thousand different pinprick silvered points looming out of the dusk. Their hopes became reflected in the shimmering silver of the newborn moon overhead.

All was calm. All was at rest.

At that moment, all was then, not painful miles of past, not miles still beyond to those distant hills. It was there, that moment, that place where they were in the wilderness. It was nowhere else. Not in Kenya, not in England, not anywhere but within themselves, within a space, a time, a place that was nowhere, but everywhere.

It reached to infinity. And somehow they touched it.

But like all illusions, the magician only kept them mesmerised for a short time. The master conjurer had to leave the stage to let them carry on with their journey.

They rested.

Out of the fading light came a caravan consisting of a man, a boy and five women, driving before them a herd of nine loaded donkeys.

"Woooooeaa!" the man called to the donkeys.

The caravan came to a halt.

"Salam! Jambo! Salam! What do we 'ave here? Well! Well! Well! Three young gents heading for Kenya. Ha! Ha! Ha!" he laughed.

"Lokichogio? A long, long way!" he

gestured.

"C'mon, pick up your bags and follow us, us, us. Ha! Ha! Ha!"

James, Nigel, and Manari went off into the dark with their new companions at a dreadfully slow pace. The donkeys, lusting for food, took to wandering from the road to forage. But always there with a ready stick to prod them on was Hahaha, the boy, or the five women.

As they traveled through the night, it was difficult to pick a course without occasionally stumbling over outcropped rocks. This made it difficult to fall asleep on their feet, though all three tried. They had walked thirty miles in the previous twenty-four hours.

Trudging on, they came to yet another small riverbed.

The little convoy moved off the road to spend the night. Thankful, they unloaded the donkeys and formed a small camp.

James, Nigel and Manari slid off to sleep ten yards away. The women made a fire, and the boy brought over a little food to share. It was some kind of grain, dry to taste, difficult to chew. It was not very appetising, but it was something.

"Thanks."

Later, the boy introduced two of the

women and tried to make conversation rather unsuccessfully. The Arabic passing between them was far from good. James gave them a precious cigarette.

"Jesus!"

To his amazement, they finished it off in five or six drags between them. They had bellows for lungs.

"Oh, oh, James. They're moving closer." said Nigel.

"Look at the breasts on them."

"Wow! What are they up to?"

"I think one of them is going to kiss me."

"Phew!" said Nigel.

"It's alright, they've stopped."

"What are they doing?"

"They're just curious and having a closer look at us in the firelight" James whispered. "They'll grow bored. See, they're moving off in a jingle of bangles and jewelry. Listen to that jingle of bangles and jewelry ...."

WEDNESDAY

Still dark, the stars pierced through the black of night, exploding outwards like bubbles rising from the surface of cooking opium. More wood was thrown on the fire, and by its light James saw the donkeys being loaded up. The itinerant band was about to hit the road.

Rising, he went over to speak to them, dismayed to find they were departing so early. But Hahaha smiled and said

"That's how it goes. We travel slow, slow, slow. You'll soon catch us up."

The boy, just before he left, gave James a heavy stick to defend himself with.

"You never know" he gestured. "Trouble can leap out from behind every bush."

And thus with this last farewell, the caravan faded into the dark.

James threw more dead wood on the fire and went back to sleep. For a twenty-two year old of his background, his life was not that of the normal average European. (Is there such a lie?) Life in the desert was far from secure. Thirst, hunger, sunburn, was

not making his life a pleasant one.
There was no future beyond the next
water hole. There seemed to be no
acceptable reasons whatsoever for
ending up in a desert. It was not
enjoyable, relaxing or idyllic.

James didn't pretend to himself that
he was there because he wished to be.
Physically it was doing nothing for him,
and mentally the experience was
twisting his mind.

He continued along his path of
dreams.

He emerged to a dawn of a shared
cigarette, a toffee to revitalise his
mouth. A piss, a crap, a brush of teeth,
a poke of ears, a scratch or two with
dirty fingers that picked a nostril before
exploring for the odd source of an
inexplicable bite. Then, the shaking of a
head to clear the dead leaves from a
knotted mass of hair as they set off on
the road again.

It was not long before the morning
sun was striking the tops of their
heads. It was a clear bright day that
chased off the cool of the night. It
brought warmth. But the heat and the
sweat that would soon follow made
them face the morning uncomfortably.

They had only gone five or six miles,
and already they were feeling the effort
of walking with their loads on their

backs. With their water low, a strong thirst overtook any thoughts they had on abstract conversation. Ahead, a band of green against the contrast of the barren wastes appeared.

The sight of a line of spreading trees raised their hopes.

"A bit of shade and water there" James concluded.

They made for the welcome protection of a banyan tree or its such, and they threw themselves to the ground in exhaustion. It was bliss to savour the pleasure of a rest from the merciless sun.

Lying back, they caught the breeze in their hands, and faces, and hair. It was so beautiful. The leaves rustled. The birds sang. The cattle lowed to the dull ring of a cowbell. Even James had the belief he could smell water.

If camels could why not men?

Nigel felt strong. He took the water bottle and went in search of the giver of life. James was beginning to realise why water was valued more than gold in the desert, and why to him it had become more desirable than wealth or food or sex and more important than hashish when in a dehydrated Saharan state of mind. It is the one thing in life midst all this vice that's wanted pure and clean and cold. The only thing to die for, but the only thing that lets us continue to live. Water. The one and only vision shimmering in the haze, a mirage, an illusion to heat crazed eyes. It brought to mind one thought only, the remembered feeling of it leveled to the lips and a thousand pleasures released in a single drop. Just one drop is enough, the rest excess, to make pleasure total and complete. The utter realisation that one drop of water sums up all the wants of human desire in one split second, that second that one drop touches the lips, trickles onto the tongue, and disperses in a million effervescent revelations of contentment. Aye. The want for nothing else except the craving to repeat the holy act for time immortal. To drink and drink and drink nature's flood, to become an aqua-vampire insatiable, until the stomach gurgles, groans and swells to say enough is enough, you drunken pig!

Amidst all this thought, James's eyelids drooped for a moment.

Hee-Haw! Hew-haw!

"What was that?" a voice in James's head cried. Opening his eyes, two of the donkey women who had been so curious the night before, were standing to his left. Their donkeys were grazing a short distance away. Nigel had still not returned and Manari was fast asleep. Manari was in a bad way. It didn't look as though he was going to make it.

James was having a hard time keeping his eyes open.

The two women stood staring, both young and in their twenties. One, hands on her hips, and the other hand in mouth, passed comments on his first James, and then Manari's appearance. Hands-on-Hips was the pretty one, her hair cropped short, her eyes flashing and enhanced by her powerful white teeth and open smile. Her neck was layered in beads and bands of multi-coloured sequences climbing loosely up her chin. Her breasts hung heavy, dark inch long nipples pushing out, inviting thoughts of long caressing nights in the lonely bush. Her hips were broad and firm enough to support a thousand child births, her thighs protruding from the leg-long slits of her hide wrap-around. Black and melting, James's eyes traveled upwards to her crotch, to where she kept her mystery, her hidden treasure, behind a small flappable piece of leather swaying, dancing, teasing at the eyes when caught in the breeze, but withholding triumphantly against any mental will to make it move. One inch more, just that tentative distance between seclusion and exposure. Yet that final frustration, her garment designed to reveal all, but the very lips of her inviting sanctuary, thus forcing the defeated eye to turn away from her black beauty ... as she looked down with a knowing smile. She had power over men, her knowledge that they would succumb to her ripe breasts, hot wanton thighs, and quiver at her flouting crotch, give her control. She could manipulate at her whim.

"My god! Where has Nigel gone? Rescue me!"

But the woman did not know her own beauty, and James was let off lightly for his spermatozoa thoughts.

"Gibrite? Gibrite?" the other woman interrupted. James was jolted out of thought.

"Oh, matches. Sure, sure" he said handing over a box with a rhinoceros on the label.

The woman gazed briefly at the rhino and commented to her friend before collecting together a few handfuls of dried up grass, striking a light, and setting half the oasis on fire.

"Bullshit!" the women scorned with laughs at James's humoured taunt.

"At least we've got something to cook on our fire!" they taunted.

"Got any for us?" James gestured.

"No" they replied, but after many no's, tuts, and wagging of fingers with mocking, heated, bickering words, they changed their minds.

"Okay. If you trade."

"Trade what?"

"Anything" they said with a wiggle of hands.

"Ah! I have it. Hold on ladies, I have the very thing!"

He rummaged in his bag.

"Here we are. I bought this in India. As a matter of fact, I had it made for me by the Singh Brothers at the Godaulla in Benares, the holy city by the River Ganges. What do you think? It's made to measure. A genuine white Indian silk waistcoat, the best you could hope to find in all of Africa! Is it a deal? Yes! Wonderful! You have made an excellent purchase. Now what do I get in exchange?"

Hand-on-Hips rushed off to reappear some minutes later with a large calabash container. Placing it on the ground in front of James, she invited him to place his hand inside.

"Heh! wait a minute, there could be a snake inside there, one of these little poisonous things or other."

"Don't be daft. Look!" the woman pointed.

"Oh no. Not those damned berries

again. That's not what you're going to trade for a fine Indian waistcoat, is it?"

"Yes" she said with a double nod.

"Christ! They're horrible. I nearly choked on them last night. Haven't you got any nice pieces of meat?"

"No" she said with a double shake.

"What! That's all you've got! Please don't tell me that's it. Berries? Bloody berries? I can't stand them. Yuck!"

"There is nothing else" Hands-on-Hips said, hands outstretched.

"Well, it's ..." James stopped short. "Nigel!"

Nigel was back with the container full of water.

Nigel woke Manari while James took the container and downed a long cool drink before passing it to Manari, now wide-awake and eager to take his turn.

"Much better" James said, turning to face the woman again. "Now, ah yes, the berries".

"Here, shall we move further into the shade" Hands-on Hips' friend suggested, inviting them over to where Hahaha, the boy and the other women were resting.

"The waistcoat for berries?" she said to the others.

The others nodded, James resignedly agreed, and it was a deal. The women handed over two kilos of berries for the waistcoat.

"Shit deal" thought James. "First a sleeping roll and now my waistcoat."

Hand-on-Hips handed the garment to Hahaha, who, horror of horrors, wrapped it around his head like a turban.

"Hmmmmmmmm........." the women sighed. "It doesn't suit you, Hahaha."

Hahaha took it off and handed it to the boy, who with the intelligence of the younger generation, slipped his arms through the appropriate sleeve spaces and tried to button the waistcoat up. But confusion took over, and frustration developed with his failure to secure a button into a buttonhole. Yet it was hardly surprising. The waistcoat was inside out.

Finally, the boy put the waistcoat on the right way. Everyone remarked how smart he looked. Indeed, it was a nice waistcoat, though James thought it rather strange to see a naked boy wearing nothing else but a white silk waistcoat while cradling a spear. Usually a brown cloth cloak draped one shoulder, and as the only garment, their long dangling penises were openly on show. Somehow, the waistcoat did not seem to blend with the more traditional mode of dress.

However, while the boy was proud of his new possession, James was not as enthusiastic about what he had got in exchange. Yet he had no choice. He was wasting away. By now, all three had used up their body reserves.

James cooked up the berries with some lentils. The lentils were fine, but the berries were dry inside which made them difficult to down. Chew. Chew. Chew. They chewed until their mouths were sore and tired. Chew. Chew. Chew.

James, in misery, ended up throwing his meal away. He made sure no-one saw him in case the tribes-people raised more than an eyelid at him throwing away good food midst desert waste.

"Ah, well, they'll never notice" he said to himself.

He finished off his cup of tea, and spread out to relax and watch the day go by. It was a pleasant rest to be enjoyed by a busy water hole. Tribesmen with long twelve-foot spears materialised out of the bush. They stopped awhile to eye them all, then moved off back into the bush. Most were serious faced, a quick uttered Jambo the nearest they came to smiling. However, to a man, they were interested in the traveler's packs.

The three wisely kept most things out of sight. It was best not to tempt the tribesmen, or let ideas ferment in their heads. Their lives could depend on that. Yet they felt reasonably assured that no one would try to steal a something from them or take a quick prod at them with their spears.

With their many cattle, the herdsmen were constantly on the move from one water hole to the next. Keeping ahead of the dry season, they drove their cattle south into Uganda or northwards into the Nile swamps. Many struck eastwards into Ethiopia and towards the Ogaden, and remained there until the next rains. Already, the land to the south was drying out. The dust was beginning to rise. The grass was burnt to its roots. The wild life was migrating and soon the semi-desert would be a burnt black waste where everything died. Only the deep rooted trees and the cacti would have any hope of surviving until the March rains came in five months time. Already, the riverbed wells had been dug dry. The tribal people had excavated sand and dirt downwards of thirty feet in the more solid riverbank, but eventually the water table had been leeched dry. The water had disappeared beneath the bedrock.

This was the sign for the last migrates that it was time to move on with their cattle. Ahead was a journey of a thousand miles. The earliest migrates would have been successful in moving south into Kenya. But now that the wells had dried out, the late migrates were forced to travel north as far as Malakal on the Nile. It was a long trek, but every year the nomads covered enormous distances in search of grazing and water for their cattle. Their sole claim to wealth was hundreds, sometimes thousands of cows and goats. The cattle were use to buy wives. They represented status. The cattle were not for milk or meat, but purely so that a man might boast of how many cows or goats he had. The more a man possessed, the more he could boast, and thus, the bigger that man became within the tribe.

With a burning ambition to own more cattle, the tribesmen would steal another man's cows and think nothing of killing another tribesman in the process. If the dead man's tribe knew who had slain their kinsman, they could demand many hundreds of cows in repayment of the death.

This was the extent of retribution. The cows and goats meant everything to the tribe. The death of an animal was mourned with tribal chants and dances. A man's animals were foremost in importance after the chief of the tribe. After all, the chief had the right to order a man's cattle to be taken from him. It was a dictatorial way of government. The tribe lived on the chief's whims. The tribe was a family living under the stern law of a god-like father.

However, the tribesmen by the water hole behaved like gentlemen. They cordially greeted one another with great respect. There was no tension. Everyone seemed to be content with what they had.

Then from nowhere, a man clothed in a light blue, red and white hooped sweater, a pair of khaki shorts, and shod in India rubber sandals, appeared. He stealthily carried a .303 rifle. On his head, cocked sideways, was a black army type beret with badge, indiscernible at such a distance.

The tribesmen froze.

The newcomer kept to the open and beckoned to a nervous tribesman sitting under a tree. The tribesman, hesitant, arose and moved towards rifleman uneasily.

They talked.

The rifleman pointed here and there. The cattle in the waterhole. The distant hills. The stretching road.

James tried to follow their conversation by watching their body movements. He harboured the nagging thought that the man would eventually get round to asking them why they were so far into the bush.

Was he a policeman? Had he heard of them?

From the reactions of the other tribesmen, James was sure the rifleman represented some form of high authority in the area. Despite what had been said back in the town, there did seem to be some kind of law and order in the desert. Whoever the chief was who laid claim to the territory they were passing through, the man with the beret was one of the men who patrolled his land. James thought it strange that he did not seem in the least interested in them. He had some larger issue on his mind.

The rifleman completed his business with the other man. With the wave of an arm, he gave the three strangers a passing greeting and then set off with a cocky swagger into the bush.

The tribesmen let out audible sighs of relief. Many of them harboured guilty consciences about past wrongdoings.

It was not surprising, close inspection of the cattle by James revealed that very few had the same brand mark as the beast closest to it. Perhaps there was belief in variety, but more likely much of the tribesmen's status had been acquired by foul means. It was perpetuated by a vicious circle of thought. If robbed, steal.

The day passed on.

James lay stretched out, watching the sun filter through the green interwoven branches overhead. Contented, he cleaned his fingernails with small twigs. He watched the small birds perch on the backs of the cows in search of ticks. Turning, he watched a tribesman hammer out his damaged spearhead with a stone, and followed the movements of a woman scraping out her pumpkin gourd. Rays of blinding light caught his eyes, and reflected off a boy looking at his youthful face in a small piece of broken mirror. In the bright sunshine, scattered shafts of blazing light threw images from the polished interfaces of the silvered glass.

It was two hours to sunset. The donkey caravan had moved off an hour before. James, Nigel, and Manari were waiting for the rising breeze to fan the air. Until such time, they sat peacefully savouring the last painless hour of rest.

With their five-litre water container filled, they anticipated they would have enough water until they reached the next waterhole.

At last, it was time. Even with the taming of the mid-day sun, the heat that hit them as they left the shade was more than they expected.

Manari, as usual, soon dropped behind.

James and Nigel met with a tribesman.

"Hello there! Jambo" they exchanged before offering their hands in friendship. The tribesman, a cheerful individual commenced with a triple action handshake.

"I see" James said, getting the hang of the tribesman's handshake.

They went through the whole exercise again. First the normal Western handshake, then the American interlocking thumbs handshake, then back to the normal handshake.

"I see" James said again. "All in one movement. One. Two. Three. Easy, eh!"

Manari, meanwhile, had caught them up.

"Heh, Manari, you want to try the African handshake?" Nigel asked him. "It's easy. One. Two. Three. Jambo."

"Ah so! Won. Too. Tree" he grinned weakly.

Nigel, in jovial mood, showed the herdsman the wrist shake, followed by the forearm shake, a combination of both which had the herdsman in fits of laughter.

"Come on, let's have a final round" Nigel shrieked in fun. "One. Two. Three. And we'll be on our way."

The herdsman grinned in understanding. One. Two. Three, he shook, and they were on their way.

The road began to stretch. It was a road that was hard, hot, and that dragged for miles. It drained and exhausted. It made sweat trickle from their brows like little springs bubbling from the surface of some hidden reservoir. It flowed down their temples to gather momentum and flood the hollows of their backs. It was a road that was hot and stretching. It made their backs salty lakes, their packs giant sponges of sodden canvas. It was a road that pushed them towards collapse.

When they finally collapsed, they panted until the unseen force, the faceless power, the gentle and the destroying, rescued them with fanning beauty, and whisked away their soggy clothes, their dampened socks, their moistened cheeks and their beaded brows with one long and lasting gust. A breeze. It shifted the clinging air to allow the freshness of early evening to invade. It conquered the sun's hold of day, and prepared them for the cool of night.

They managed to drag themselves another weary mile. They pulled to the top of a steep rise, exhausted and all in. They threw themselves and their packs into one tired pile.

Glugging from the water container, they stared upwards at the waxing moon. All of a sudden, Manari began to throw up, and when James and Nigel had got a brushwood fire together, they discovered he had thrown up blood. He lay doubled up in a fever, while they built up the fire to keep the cheetahs and hyenas at bay.

They cooked some lentil soup on the blaze, and offered some to Manari, but he was too weak and in too much pain to eat. James and Nigel, beyond all conversation, stacked the fire with more dead wood, and crashed out to the echoes of some haunting bird. Both knew what was going to happen, both had seen the same thing back in the town.

The disease struck everyone the same way. By morning, Manari would be dead.

THURSDAY

Dawn.

The only pleasant time of day to walk. Everything so still and silent, the shadow of death followed their constant, continual grating steps. Here and there a loose stone producing a short stumble, or a short dragging of feet. Then back to Crunch! Crunch! Crunch! Endless yards turning to miles, as maggots, flies, ants and scavenging birds ate the flesh from Manari's body left behind.

They could do little else beyond bury his body beneath brushwood and rocks a little before dawn. He had died, as they knew he would, the disease spared no one. It was crazy that they had been caught in the area at the time of the outbreak. Having broken the quarantine, they were recaptured and placed under house arrest. They had traveled two hundred miles from Juba where they had been initially quarantined with natives in a camp, a camp where all suspected victims of the disease had been brought not to be treated, but to die. No one really knew what was going on, what the disease was, or how it could be cured.

James and Nigel had been ushered

into the camp almost by gunpoint, and had met Manari, the only other foreigner, isolated in a corner, trying to dissociate himself from the natives. The little Jap spoke very little English, and had seemed utterly bewildered with his situation. Through Manari's Japanese/English dictionary, James had tried to explain all he knew about the situation, and had indicated that he and Nigel were getting out of there as fast as they could. Manari wanted to go along.

After paying off the guard and arranging a ride on the back of a supply truck, they had managed to get two hundred miles further east towards the Kenyan border, until they fell into the hands of the police in the town at the end of the road. Still eighty miles from the Kenyan frontier, they had been placed under arrest for breaking the quarantine.

However, no one in the town wanted anything to do with them, just in case they had actually caught the disease. The police didn't want them in the cells; it was too close for comfort. Instead, they housed them in a bungalow, and restricted their movement in the town.

After nine days and the threat of being sent back to where they had come from, they had taken off into the bush towards Kenya. The rest you know.

So now the disease had claimed Manari, the disease that almost dropped a man overnight without prior warning. The sort of disease that was common in Africa, the type no one else in the world heard about, except those afflicted. Africa, the Dark Continent, the bad health gutter of the world. The testing ground for subtle germ warfare by the super powers. Isolated tribal Africa, where no news entered or escaped, the most primitive continent on the globe. Sure, it was all right to test out a new strain of germ on the nomads of Central Africa, no one would ever get to know.

But James knew, he was intelligent enough to work out things for himself, as the rubber on the soles of his boots met rock and slowly burnt up. The rubber disintegrating a hundred thousandth of an inch at a time - on torturous friction singeing granite, flint and igneous rock. Grinding, gorging rocks, ripping deep, inflicting soul-destroying damage. A damage unseen, but not unfelt. A damage that results in huge inflated ballooning blisters full of yellow pus.

The blisters plagued their feet. They had taken their turn with the darning needle to painfully puncture each aquatic sore. Fountains like thundering geysers arced skywards, then fell earthwards to shower everything in near proximity with a sticky pungent fluid. The initial inrush of air stung horribly before they could squeeze out the remaining pus. Quickly they dabbed each blister with a cloth or sock or whatever came to hand before the sand flies settled. An application of a band aid, the replacement of a sock, preceded the lacing up of a boot.

Then that reluctant first step which took them back on the road and away forever from the spot where they had been too inadequate to give their friend a decent burial. What use were words over the dead. Within a week, his body and soul would be scattered across the desert in the faeces of a vulture, or carried on a sand blown wind.

What was the difference?

Manari had been a Buddhist, but to burn his body on the fire was too disgusting a thought for James to even mention to Nigel. No, they had done the decent thing and covered his body with brush and rocks as best they could.

Still the road stretched on.
They held their heads up, and

walked a few surprisingly easy going miles. They took in the view offered by the pitch and roll of the worn way before they hit a soft dirt patch that helped to give their feet a more cushioned ride. Then it was back to flint and limestone.

In the not too far distance, a band of green stretched away from the road. Their steps quickened as thoughts of shade, and of a cool wet well spurred them on. Over one rise and down a slope. Over another rise, getting nearer. Still more rises and dips, almost there, just a few more steps.

"I see the river bed and can hear the sound of cattle." James told himself. "Look, a band of leafy trees and lush vegetation. What's that?"

James fixed his gaze.

Ahead, a group of twenty brown cloaked, spear-carrying tribesmen were assembled, crouching, standing and sitting on a tree stump, huddled around the dying embers of a smoldering fire. Turning one by one to stare, the tribesmen watched the strangers approach, their attention fixed, their bodies' motionless. Their cloaks were wrapped loosely around them, catching the breeze to flutter and add life to an otherwise still shot scene.

The tribesmen broke from their

trance and stepped forward to greet James and Nigel.

"Jambo. Jambo" they said in half admiration, shaking James and Nigel's hands like old friends. Single, triple, whatever took their fancy. Strong, shy, forceful, courteous, slapping, honest handshakes.

James and Nigel were rather surprised to see so many tribesmen together.

"Are we in Kenya?" James asked them, but it took the even greater surprised tribesmen about ten minutes to get over the excitement of meeting two white men, unescorted, so far into the wasteland they inhabited.

"Kenya?" they finally answered. "No. Sudan."

James and Nigel were disappointed. On seeing half a dozen slurp thirsty cows drinking the water bubbling up from midst a mud hole, James went to fill the near-empty water container. A concerned tribesman was quick to point out that the cows were pissing and dropping shit in the water hole.

James put the cap back on the container, and tried to hide his disappointment.

One young tribesman, his black-cropped hair patted down with brick red mud in an African perm, spoke a little

English taught to him by missionaries in Kenya. He offered to take them to good water.

He trudged them off, thirsty mouthed, along a dried up riverbank. He led them through thorn thickets, under low slung branches, past a group of late rising natives, past a camp of mud huts fenced by thorns, and back down into the gravel-sand river bed. They skirted fallen flood-washed trees, and tried to find the hardest, supporting, easiest to walk on sand, until at last, around a long curving bend, they stopped.

The tribesman made James and Nigel stare down a twenty-foot hole. At the bottom was a well that reflected their faces in its water.

A small crowd of natives gathered, and one man volunteered to slide down the hole and fill their water container. He passed it up so they could drink the life giving liquid that soon put a little life back into their shrinking stomachs. Having had their fill, they took shade under the protecting branches of a tree spanning half way across the river bed, their English speaking friend squatting down beside them, to tell them that it was still forty-two miles to Lokichogio, the first village in Kenya.

"Forty-two!" Nigel looked at him in

despair. "I reckon we've done fifty. We were told it was seventy miles to Lokichogio."

"That means it should only be twenty more miles" added James.

"No, I am sorry. Kappoeta is forty-four miles from here and Lokichogio forty-two."

"That doesn't add up, that's sixteen more than we were told." Nigel was cracking up. Despite his bursts of energy, his hepatitis was eating away his liver. He needed sugar if he was to get better. All he was getting was water.

They had mentioned nothing about Manari or the disease to the tribesman.

"Why don't they have milestones in this ..." James checked himself.

"Sorry, that was a stupid think to say."

"Forget it!" Nigel shrugged.

They were both deflated. They had thought that they might have spent the rest of the day by the coolness of the waterhole. But now, with the end so physically distant, they could only afford to rest for an hour.

An hour passed, two, before they retraced their steps back along the riverbed to the road. Back by curving bend, soft sand, washed out trees, gravel bed, mud huts, yawning natives, low-slung branches, thorn thickets.

The tribesmen who earlier in the day had been gathered by the cattle-hole had gone. The only trace of their existence was a smoldering fire.

Thirsty mouthed, they trudged on.

The sun rose higher. The pointer on James' thermal thermometer headed for the red line. His limit of tolerance had been reached. He had long passed the line of bare ability. He had entered into the zone of torture, masochism. He had reached the zone where mental cruelty to the body was justified for long-term gain. The zone it rarely reaches, sacrifice. The zone where the coming pain has not been previously experienced. The point where the mind believes the body to be a mere machine that can withstand great neglect. A machine that is expected to operate at the same working level at all times.

When the mind becomes confused, it can forget that the body can buckle in the heat. Parts of the body can warp. The body can overheat and then fail to function.

The mind can make great mistakes of judgment. Past information may be useless. With nothing to relate to, it can become a new experience for mind and body, a new test of co-operation between management and machine.

James was developing no close harmony for success. His body was warping. He was struggling to triumph and finally overcome everything, the heat, the lack of food and the scarcity of water. Yet something in him made him want to defeat the odds, to force through the self-imposing barriers that inhibit. An inner voice spoke to him. Persevere! Forge on!

His own voice uttered. Oh! My head. My head.

Nigel, in a newfound strength, led the way. Keeping up a steady pace, he would disappear round twisting curves of matted bush, James getting glimpses of his back through prickly thorn scrub.

Keeping Nigel just in sight, a careering, fleeting figure, leaving treaded tell-tale tennis shoe steps on the sandy road; James stumbled on in forced pursuit.

"I hope to God he stops for a rest" James mulled. "Just a small stop over. But no, on he goes, widening the gap between us, stretching it with his every step. The hollows of inviting shade offered by these leafless trees tempt me. But I must resist. This nagging desire to halt could be the end of me. I must deny myself cool respite from this oppressive heat. I must struggle on."

He wiped salty sweat from his forehead, his forearms streaked rivers of streaming tide marked dirt - hands clammy, sticky, clenched - bare brown legs scratched and scratched by brushing barbs from lurking thorns. His chest heaving, stomach tightening, visions of a never ending walk to eternity going on and on, mile after half hour mile. And always the hope that around each twist or curve would be the sight of Nigel lounging, sprawled in desert comfort - off the road - lying in some sheltered, sun-escaped oasis.

Four miles.

That was all, before James joined Nigel in the sanctuary of a shady little haven. He dropped solidly, in one throwing movement, into the filtered shadows cast by a towering leafless bush.

Nigel passed the water.

"Just a capful now" he reminded James.

James stared vacantly at his own sprawled out legs.

"This heat is killing me" he said in all seriousness. "I reckon if I didn't have this hat, I'd be dead by now."

He glanced at Nigel, a green towel held on his head by a red bandanna, in Arabian style.

"You're a joke with that on your

head" he managed to laugh.

James played with the tassels of his own straw hat. Nigel, rubbed his hand in the sand, and looked up and smiled, before something made him glance along the road, the sunlight forcing him to look down.

Trying again, he couldn't quite make out what it was that had caught his attention. He thought he had seen Manari, though he was not quite sure as he was forced to look away again. Third time lucky, he made out the thing to be an anthill.

It was amazing how anthills took on all shapes.

"Remember the thirty foot tall ones, back in Kappoeta?" James half asked, half recalled.

They were really something. All that earth piled into one large column like a chimney-stack, tons upon tons of earth collected into one giant edifice by thousands, no, millions of tiny insects smaller than a fingernail. Tiny little creatures swarming, marching, locating, gathering grain by grain, all that shit. Soldiers fighting off attackers, the workers designing, constructing, placing each tiny load, each mass of their collected building material into one massive tower of offices, homes, restaurants, prisons, barracks, maternity hospitals, a whole city of seething, communal, kibbutzy ants, living together for safety and convenience. Warring with their neighbours, conquering, keeping slaves of a different colour or cast to do the dirty work. A complete society, hatching, living, dying - perpetual procreation lasting ant generations, surviving flooding in the wet, famine in the dry, human intervention at all times. Until the day the structure walls irreparably crumble and decay, it's life span at an end, the structured city as a whole, unsafe to inhabit. Until the leader ants take a decision, a slow ponderous one, to lay the eggs in a new store in preparation for a colony in sight of the old. Then followed on by a mass exodus, perhaps an adventure of marching off into the wilds in search of a new home, the old and weak left behind, only the strong and determined expected to survive. A band of pioneers in search of a new land, a new horizon, a new beginning. That hard rewarding place of rest for the survivors, where skirmishes with hostile colonies are imminent, total annihilation or subjective slavery their fate. But the will to live, keeping the loyal band of adventurers united, until their final march is over, and the next generation hatched, carries the spirit of their ancestors by committing themselves to building another towering monument to grace the African skyline.

James was off in this escape, when suddenly; Nigel was up on his feet. There was no time to lose. Nigel felt life ebbing away.

"God! Not already" James moaned.

But Nigel was up and staring down at James. "Just a mile or two, that's all. I'm nearly finished too."

James gazed up through hazy, reluctant eyes.

Nigel set off. "I'll see you soon!"

There was just no rest.

James pulled himself together, took another capful of water, tottered to his feet, squared to the road, pulled his straw hat down to shade his eyes, and waddled unsteadily on his blisters. Feeling his strength returning, his step quickened. His adrenaline surged around his body, and the road became just another city street in need of being swept. Then the sun, the ever draining, the ever stabbing sun, impacted.

WHOOOOOMPH!

Every laboured step became more difficult than the last. James turned his thoughts to death. He dropped. He submitted to the sun's direct rays.

Then he noticed tyre tracks, fresh and newly traced in the sand.

A Land Rover?

But they were double tracks. Immediately James got on his knees and prayed.

"Please God, no" he said.

The Land Rover had been driven that far into the bush, then turned around.

With his mind completely occupied, James hauled himself up and wandered on midst his deductions until his attention was sharply brought back to focus by a fully grown, large horned bushbuck. It shot across the road barely five yards in front.

"Good grief! Phew! No sweat" he said, taking it in his stride. He was past shock.

The sun was really getting to him. The only saving grace was a slight wafting breeze that kept him from boiling over. The flies buzzed his eyes, his ears, his lips, and tried to climb into his nostrils.

"No" he cried suddenly, "I don't believe it, it's a mirage!"

To his left, the wavy tyre track marks headed off into the bush and ended at a green topped, yellow number plated land rover. By it stood two bare-chested, bush-hatted, pitch black Africans.

They beckoned to him.

"Kenyans!"

Yippee! Rescue! No more walking and a comfortable ride to Lokichogio. Yippee! Stuff you, you fucking old miserable sun. Stuff you! And Nigel? I see Nigel sprawled out in the shade of the land rover. You're real, and I can't suppress this cheery smile on my face.

The Africans rushed forward. They briefly shook his hand. They handed him a lidless coca-cola can full of water, and apologized

James drank the water.

"What is this? They are sorry? What's going on? They feel bad about the situation? What do they mean? I'm the one that's feeling bad, but it's happened now and there is nothing to be done. Would someone like to explain the whole thing to me? Nigel?"

Nigel clasped his hands, dejected. He was like a man whose time had come to make confession before climbing the steps to the gallows.

"I'm sorry." His first words stuck James. They were released with a sighing hiss of regret.

"Sorry for what? Tell me, don't keep me waiting."

"They've run out of petrol."

James heard someone screaming

from inside his mind, and shook his head, but the screaming echoed on and on, until at last it was lost midst other voices, strange bub-a-lop voices, speaking broken English.

"Are you alright, man? Hey are you alright?"

"Yes, yes, they're asking me if I'm alright."

James opened his eyes and saw the two black Africans standing over him. They looked concerned.

"You fainted, man. Are you sure you're alright?"

James nodded.

He was helped into the shade of a bush. A car cushion was placed under his head, as both men looked down on him worriedly. Nigel was splayed out just as helpless, panting, heaving and sweating. Neither of them had little thought for anything else except water.

Gathering enough strength, James dragged himself under the chassis of the Land Rover. He was exhausted and unable to move.

So this was what happened to modern day adventurers. Their adventure had turned to a nightmare journey of endless torturous miles. It was cracking the hard-core heads of each of them. It was pulling them piece by piece apart. It had killed Manari.

The very life that made them what they were ... a pair of windblown tumbleweeds, confessed dope freaks, anti-authoritarians living by their own decisions, politely flirting in and out of conventional social scenes of all forms, learning, picking up weird habits, ideas from weirder experiences, trying to keep the action at a high pitch level ... it was killing them. Where was that quiet spot to try a little meditation, contemplation, general relaxation, with a little help from hash or grass? Where was the peace and rest, the no hassle zooting trouble free life of a seat outside a little restaurant, tucked around a nearby corner, to watch the world go by?

All these little niceties were a long way off from where their bodies now were strewn.

Yet the choice had been theirs. They had known the risks, the coming discomforts involved before they undertook to walk for freedom. They had expected difficulties, setbacks, physical pain. They had figured the odds. They had accepted them, and still accepted them. The ordeal was a chance to show themselves that they could survive against all the odds. Back in Kappoeta, a few sympathetic souls had advised them against setting off. They had heard nothing but "It can't be done" since they had first thought of crossing the desert.

And now, the final test, the deed half done, their will to carry on was a little weaker. Yet still they were determined to carry on until they dropped. They refused to die like Manari.

Well, they had dropped all right, but the human body and brain is flexible enough to overcome simple faints, lack of food and shortage of water. Vertigo, malnutrition, dehydration, they were not real things to worry about. There was much more than that.

The disease. The Green Monkey that; gave a high fever, headache, back pain, tightness in the chest, and abdominal pain. Followed by a cough, blood-stained-sputum and diarrhea with blood in the stools, bleeding from the nose and mouth, vomiting of blood, and a rapid deterioration due to dehydration. A disease that was like typhoid fever, but which in fact was a virus disease. A disease that generally killed within seven days, but frequently killed within twenty-four hours.

The sun went down.

Kimba and Marka prepared a meal of goat meat and rice.

James and Nigel were rallied enough

to scrape the flesh from every ridge, crack and knob of bone. They dug with trembling fingers into a mountain of hot, heavy rice, which was so hard to swallow; their throats ached with use. They were out of practice when it came to eating. Neither of them had had a decent meal for fifteen days.

The rice bounced down their gullets to fill their bellies with a long vacant warmth. After a while, an overflowing contentment oozed out to relieve their tired bodies. They were full, but Marka handed a mug of maize-meal porridge to them.

"Porridge!" James heard himself exclaim in his own head. "Who would believe it in the heat of the desert. Heh! Kimba!"

"Yes my friend? Porridge? Ha! Porridge is very good for you. We call it ooja in Swahili. Listen, friends. Tomorrow I have to walk to Kappoeta. It is a long story why we ran out of petrol, but I shall tell you........."

James and Nigel were curious to know how the two men had ended up stranded in the middle of the bush. There was something covert in their behaviour.

"As you know" Kimba began "the frontier has been closed because of this terrible disease. However, we have business commitments in the Sudan that we must honour. We had to make special arrangements with the authorities so we could pass through here. However, at Lokichogio, the police stopped us, and turned us back. They said we should go back to the good life in Nairobi. Fortunately, Marka knew the local government official, who told us of another road which skirted around Lokichogio and the mountains to come out on the Sudan road on the other side of the border."

Kimba grinned.

"Well, the border itself is just a dried up river bed. There is no checkpoint between Lokichogio and Kappoeta. It was simple. We took the mountain road last night, thinking that the detour would be no more than ten-fifteen miles, but as it's turned out, it was nearly fifty. Just as dawn was breaking, we ran out of petrol. We knew we were short, but not that short."

Kimba turned serious.

"Anyway, the detour has finished us. We spent all our money on buying the merchandise."

He nodded to a large tarpaulin wrapped bundle on the roof of the land rover.

"We need to sell our load in Sudan."

There was something in the way he spoke which suggested that they were involved in some sort of trafficking. Kimba couldn't hide it.

"Just in case the police sent out a patrol to find us, we pushed the land rover off the track and into the bush here where you have found us. And now ... I have to walk to Kappoeta to fetch some petrol."

The mention of Kappoeta made James sick.

"Marka will stay here. We can't go back to Lokichogio; the police will lock us up. I know I am going to suffer walking to Kappoeta, as you have suffered, but I know I shall make it. The last time my car broke down in the bush, I had to walk sixty-three miles. I walked and walked, rarely stopping, and made it after two days. But for days later I could not move, my legs refused to work. It was all very painful, but I did it."

Kimba's pride swelled up like a balloon. James and Nigel exchanged glances.

"And now I must do the same again. Fifty miles you say. It is far, but if I walk day and night I can do it in just over a day. I will suffer, how I think now, I will suffer. But it is not as bad for me, I'm used to the heat, I've no bag to carry like you have - I'm used to walking."

Doesn't he go on and on, James thought. But he was too tired to reply. And anyway, maybe he was right.

"Tomorrow morning I will set off. I shall be back in three days with a truck, or if not that, a bicycle. I can strap a petrol can to the frame and push the bicycle along as I ride another."

"I don't know about that" Nigel said. "It isn't a road. Its rough rock strewn country all the way."

"Doesn't matter" Kimba replied. "If you wish, you can remain here until I return. We have plenty of food. Marka will see that you eat well. Both of you are very weak. Perhaps it would be better if you both drove to the Sudanese town with us, instead if risking your lives by walking on to Lokichogio. It's thirty-odd miles of desert with no water on the way. All the water holes are dry. Maybe I could do it, but you are both very weak. It would be much safer if you stayed here until I returned. After some more time in the Sudan, maybe they will reopen the frontier, and we can all drive to Nairobi together."

Nairobi? What a beautiful word. A golden sound to James's ear. The thought of returning to Kappoeta raised the word defeat in James's head.

Likewise Nigel. He'd had enough of Kappoeta too. He had set his heart on reaching Kenya, and had no desire to retrace his steps over the tear jerking miles they'd already walked. Such an action would have made it all for nothing. To return to another indeterminable wait in the town, possible prosecution by the police for escaping, would no doubt result in them being escorted back to Juba, disease and jail.

No, it all seemed too risky. There was more to lose by going backwards, and all to gain by pushing on. It was only thirty miles to Lokichogio. They could do it. They knew they could. Two more days and they were through into Kenya.

Kimba took their answer.

"Then stay one more day and rest before you carry on. If you do this, then I believe you can do it."

James and Nigel agreed.

Rising from his crouched position, Kimba said goodnight. He left them to the crackling fire and the silence of the stars. They lay wearily watching the flames until their senses dulled, and deep dreamless sleep overtook their conscious world of dust, dusk and dark.

FRIDAY

It was the last day of October.

By first light, it was Halloween in England. The people four thousand miles away were cutting faces out of hollowed turnips and pumpkins.

Kimba started off on his long solo journey. With him he took two empty quart bottles of Vat 69, filled with water, one gripped tightly in each hand. He was dressed rather casual for the trek ahead. His string vest exposed his broad black shoulders. His grey striped trousers were rolled up to just below his knees. His shoes were loosely tied, heels worn, toes scraped and coated in a layer of dust.

Turning as he left, he gave a fleeting grinning smile, clinked the bottles together in a last salute and then disappeared into the black enveloping bush.

Marka watching him go, threw a branch of dead wood on to the smoldering fire, and thickened up some porridge for breakfast.

The day began very slowly. They took great care to go easy on the water. They sat around and chased off the flies. They poked at the ground with twigs to make random shapes that represented nothing. They moved into the shade as the sun crept skywards. They waited to crawl under the land rover as the fiery orb stretched towards its zenith.

It was hot.

At times it was stifling, and James felt his inner soul and breath being sucked away from him. The occasional gust of wind brought a shower of sand that wafted his sweating temples, and cooled his gaping mouth.

All conversation with Nigel was casual and rambling, and mostly reflective of their ordeal. Their breakfast of porridge, sifted maize meal and heated water was simple, wholesome, basic food, which Nigel praised highly. He swore that they would have pissed the walk had they carried a couple of kilos of the meal......

James only listened with half an ear. He sighed and made a stifled moan about the heat. England became his dream. He nodded, dozed and then fell asleep, even though he tried hard to remain awake. He was too weak to fight, and finally he succumbed.

Marka meanwhile kept to himself. His English was very poor, his thoughts a secret hidden in Swahili. He had a mute smile which, although always warm and encouraging, did not detract from his eyes. His eyes were always lost within a maze of tunnels somewhere else.

The sun beat down.

At last, dusk approached. It came slowly. It took James and Nigel quite awhile to emerge from their side less shade-hole beneath the Land Rover. Marka sliced some meat, and they fed on lamb as the sun set on the hills to the west, and died.

To the hungry boys, the lamb tasted good. The rice was thick and filling, and a cup of cherished lukewarm water chased away the rest of their cares.

Marka pulled out from behind the rear seat of the land rover a portable radio-record player. He laid it on the ground and tuned into Radio Kampala, Uganda.

Weird, natty-dread, pseudo Rasta-man music floated over the cactus, scrub, and burnt bush. Paul Simon's *Mother and Child Reunion* started to happen right there in the middle of the dry African desert. It changed uninviting bush into a swaying, moving, jive-hyped, uncontrollable dancing beauty that was partnered by a raving, flamboyant, young redheaded fire. Like a nymph, the fire was a lightning footed dancer with synchronized body movements, whip-lashing to every note crackling out of the radio. The fire was the undisputed centre of attraction, it's fiery gown of cobalt and swirling potassium dancing in the evening breeze. James sat in admiration of it alone, as the final hanging chords of Simon's song, the last hovering note, suspended motionless like a halo above the fire which reached up with a cold white arm to clutch it, and PUFFFFFF!.

The music was gone. It disappeared in a heated wave of violent sulphur and copper hews as the radio crackled in some unknown Ugandan language.

The desert night returned.

The desolation closed in once more, as Halloween went on in England.

SATURDAY

With sunrise an hour away and sleep still dragging on their eyelids, James and Nigel shook hands with Marka.

They set off into the grey of dawn, their packs rubbing their rested, though still bruised shoulders. Their varied gaits sent their bobbing heads in different rhythmic action.

James occupied his mind by thinking of Marka and the merchandise on top of the land rover. He had caught a glimpse of what lay beneath the tarpaulin draped loosely over to conceal it. He knew why Kimba and Marka had made their detour around the frontier post. The business they were in called for under-handedness and secrecy.

James was not a moralist. He reminded himself that he was in Africa. When he made his discovery, he had told Nigel. Both agreed that it was none of their business. The world revolved with or without their judgments. Kimba and Marka had saved them from dying. As far as James was concerned, he had decided to forget what Kimba and Marka were smuggling out of Kenya. He owed them a favour by remaining silent. The ivory hunters had done him well.

Mile after mile; the sparse lifeless vegetation stretched monotonously. Mile after mile, the accustomed slack dead bush and odd sentinel tree became a *deja vu* of the previous mile. Nothing changed for mile after mile. The only aspect that changed was the mountain range that loomed out of the distance. They were getting nearer the barren lifeless yellow mountains.

Beyond these mountains lay Kenya.

Their efforts to walk, made conversation a chore. They walked side-by-side saying little. There was an eerie silence. The only sounds were those of their short strides and the water bottle, half full and hanging over a shoulder, slapped against Nigel's side.

When was the water container last full, James wondered? He gazed at the mountains ahead. Behind those jagged mountains lay Lokichogio, coke-cola, ice cream, gallons of cold milk. Once more, he began to fantasize, as the sun seemed to soar higher with each step forward.

Both were beginning to suffer. James couldn't get his mind off Daedalus's warning to Icarus. It was a silly thing to fix his thoughts on. He had no waxwings to melt. Yet at the back of his mind was the hope that he would live to see the way out of the maze and to escape the Minotaur.

James prayed to be spared the pains of overbearing heat, the passing miles of a living nightmare, the mental anguish, the wondering uncertainty, the wondering whether what was happening was really happening.

Were the hazy mountains up ahead veering any closer? Could he in the face of such a destroying, burning furnace, continue to strive step by step mechanically onwards?

His body was dowsed in sweat. His body was crying out for rest. His mind was forcing every limb perpetually to keep moving.

Then, something snapped in his body. His head buckled. His eyes glazed.

He barely had time to search for a shaded spot. He swayed, and almost stumbled as he made a bee-line for a piece of shade. He crashed through jagged thorns, scratching bush, to fall, trip, keel over into encompassing folds of deep cool shadow, where he lay panting, moaning, crying out in sheer vexation at the situation, wishing only to be forever in a crumpled heap.

He was ready to renounce all. We wished for nothing else but death. His brain was a total blank. Yet he was still cognate enough to know that something, somewhere was wrong. But he couldn't think straight. It couldn't be true. This couldn't be the end. This couldn't be the infinite extent of human endurance. How could this be the final giving in to all the forces out to cripple, to maim, to kill the defeated spirit. Was his body shriveled and willing to submit to utter defeat? Irrevocably? The preterit succumbing to the elements of which they should be masters?

No, it was not the end. Tiredness, malnutrition, dehydration was all it was. James had to carry on.

"For Gods sake, we've got to carry on!" screamed Nigel.

They rested an hour. Some of their strength returned. It was two hours to midday. Nigel decided that they had to move on as their water was low.

"At our present pace we'll never make it." he moaned.

Nigel was in a bad way too. He awoke James with a nudge.

"We've got to go."

It took some coaxing to agree. Finally, James nodded his head in submission.

Weary legged, hotheaded, they left the pain of another mile or two behind them. The mountains edging in on either side, drew closer. Sparse mottle green-leaved trees shielded the rocky slopes.

James and Nigel with cross-fingered wishing hoped to find water there. This thought spurred their legs over the dividing wilderness. The rocky waste broke out into grassy rolling land. The road sloped gently down towards the fertile, vegetated region of a river bed.

Heavy breathed and exhausted, they reached the riverbed. They threw their packs off and rested. Nigel, overtaken by thirst, struggled with the water container, took a swig, a gulp, until in a rush of water; the container was almost drained, their water gone...........

Nigel, now impatient and desperate, jumped into the dried up river bed, and crazily ran off in hope of finding water. James lay motionless.

Five minutes passed.

Suddenly, an almighty shout made James sit bolt upright.

"He must have found water" James told himself.

He was delirious. He began to ramble.

"Boy am I glad of that. I might as well celebrate."

James drank the remaining water in untold relief.

Nigel came running just as James

was licking the last drop of water out of the container. Nigel looked crazed.

James went into hysterics.

"You didn't find water!"

"No" screamed Nigel. He showed James a cup of sand.

James looked at Nigel, and knew there was something else wrong.

"What's the matter with you?"

"Christ, man! I've just been bitten by a snake."

"My God!" James cried, "Where?"

"My right leg. Look!" Nigel showed him a spot on his calf. The area around the bite had already swollen considerably within a few minutes.

"The pain's killing me, I can feel it traveling up my leg. I'm going to die."

"Quit talking like that", James snapped. He was scared.

"I'm going to die, I'm telling you. Give me some water."

"I've drunk the last of the water."

"What!" stuttered Nigel?

He grabbed the container.

"When you shouted, I thought you had found water."

He threw the container away in disgust. "I found all the hole dry. The last one I checked out ... there was a snake. Shit! It was lurking in the shade. The thing lashed out at me! Caught me on the leg."

"This is a nightmare!" James despaired.

"I'm not going to last out the day."

"Quit talking like that", James threatened. "Quit talking."

"Okay, okay, but I know I've had it."

James collected the container out of the riverbed and unscrewed the cap, and placed it to Nigel's mouth. A single saving drop dripped out onto his parched tongue. With a crazed eye, Nigel peered far into the empty void, searching, trying to locate a further merciful droplet. But there was no drop creeping snail-like down the yellow plastic side of the container to hover on the concave neck. No single glistening molecule of water with elongated tail stretching out elastically then suddenly recoiling on its minute body to propel itself down the throat of a dying man.

James watched as Nigel, wretched faced, replaced the cap.

"Well, we'll have to spend the rest of the day here" James said. He was trying to come to terms with what Nigel had said. Perhaps he was going to die after all.

"It's too hot to go on."

"I suppose so" Nigel said in total resignation. The poison was creeping along his blood stream.

"At least there's plenty of shade

here."

"Yeah" Nigel said without much conviction.

"We'll make it" James lied.

"Sure" Nigel replied. "But if we … you don't find water somewhere?"

"Shut up, will you".

"I'm just worried, that's all. I mean, well.......... I'm going to be all right. I don't have anything more to worry about".

"Shut up! I don't want to die out here."

James was really scared.

"I didn't say that you were going to die, did I?"

Nigel laughed like a madman.

"Look at us" he said.

He laughed again, like a man who no longer had to worry about the future.

"Do you think we're in any condition to be attending a nice fancy wedding."

"What are you on about, eh?"

"Nothing ... At least I can forget about the police, the disease, and all that. I knew all along we'd never make it."

"Stop it" James screamed. He grabbed Nigel by the throat and began to squeeze the last life out of him. Nigel, utterly crazed, tried to laugh until James, disgusted with him, threw him aside.

"I told you to shut up!"

Nigel gasping, struggled in the heat to recover his breath.

"I'm sorry!" James broke down.

"I'm sorry too. It's the heat and the pain. It's almost too much for me to take any more. I'm beginning to get scared of dying."

Suddenly Nigel began to realise that he had very little time left.

"What's there to be scared of" he said to himself.

James had no answers.

"Everything." Nigel said. "The fact that I'll never get the chance to drink another beer, screw another woman, or take any more drugs for kicks. I'm scared that I'm losing everything that I've ever enjoyed in life. I've enjoyed life so far. At twenty-one I'm supposed to be reaching the prime of life, not dying".

"Shit!" James cried "Life isn't that good. Look at me. I wish I'd been the one bitten! That's the easy way out! I don't think I'm going to make it out of this wasteland!"

"Don't talk like that. Don't lie down and wave the world goodbye. Life's too good to throw away like a paper bag."

"Is that what I'm doing?" James asked. "Look, Nig, just don't tell me you're scared. It puts the wind up me."

"Aren't you scared?"

"Sure. I don't want to be in this effin' situation." Suddenly his mood changed. "Any moment now I'm expecting some crazy flag waving American newspaper man to come charging out of the bush. In a safari suit and cork sun hat? Followed by a caravan of natives. Bearing rations and waving knives? He'll come boldly marching up, cheesy grin right across his face ... doff his hat ... shake my hand ... and using the immortal words of a well known predecessor, make himself famous at our expense."

"Crap!" Nigel said through the pain. "He'd get his story, then piss off, leaving you to the lions and mosquitoes."

"Yea, this stinks."

"I'd much prefer to be tucked away in a little pub in Leeds somewhere."

"Leeds?" James mocked.

"And what's wrong with Leeds?"

"Nothing, not a thing."

"I'd rather be there than here" Nigel said.

Suddenly they were returned to their hostile surroundings.

"Yeah" James said, noticing that Nigel was growing more and more delirious.

But Nigel didn't answer; he was in too much pain to talk any more.

It was a slow torturous afternoon. The flies zoomed in like diving stukas. Squadron after squadron loomed out of the insect darkened sky. To skip. To hop. To land cargoes of unseen filth and fly manure, before taking off to drop a load on some other part of their sweat drenched bodies.

Nigel received the worst of it. The sweetness of his infected blood attracted hoards of winged vampires. Like a plague they descended on tossing, writhing, heap struck Nigel. From every angle, they drew on his arms, his calves. They punctured the skin behind his knees. They sucked, moved on, then sucked afresh, until bloated out and gorged. The insects' desire insatiably for his saccharine saturated fluid. Nigel defending as best he could. In the end crying out.........

The roller coaster sun moving across the sky soon obliterated the adequate shade beneath the riverbank foliage. James, now alone in the desert, wriggled and crawled away from Nigel's insect swarmed body. To escape the torment of the heat, he curled himself into a ball, an arcing C, a knee-hugging

V, a horizontal Z, a tree supporting L, until at last the lengthening rays permitted a sprawling Y and X, a head resting I and a stretching T.

At last, sunset came.

As the final rays sank behind the western mountains, James finished covering Nigel's body. He had buried him in the soft sands of the dried up riverbed.

Blood mouthed, he turned from the small mound and set out on the road towards Kenya. The miles in front were tinged with uncertainty. A strong breeze sprung up and slightly erased the memory of the previous scarring hours. It lifted him from the cruelty of the day.

He struggled on. When his nose began to bleed, he was no longer counting miles. Step upon faltering step acted as his only mental measurement of the distance covered.

The evening moon guided him through the wilderness of the windy night, a night of craving thirst, unknown hunger, abject consciousness, a night of physical exhaustion, crippled senses, deranged mind. Yet still he possessed a will to carry on. He saw his silvery shadow as a signal to soldier blindly on. Somehow he managed. The mountains, once so beyond his sleeping eyes now towered, reared, climbed skywards overhead. They blotted, smothered out the candle flickering, winking stars. They created a void of empty black, punctured here and there by a jagged grey of lunar light-lit rock.

Then suddenly, James let out a choking cry.

"Enough!"

He wavered off the road, and in a half twist-backward horizontal- roll, crumpled on to a makeshift bed of bruising stones and spiky thorns. There he lay until he summoned up enough dying strength to collect some firewood.

Striking up a blaze, tales of gruesome wild animal stories sped through his mind. Then for a moment, staring at the flames, he imagined the fleeting figure of the dancing lady, alive and whispering 'Come with me'........

Yet, still half awake, his dreams were cruelly haunted by the want for water. He imagined himself in a shower, lying on the floor with mouth agape, the torrent sweeping down. But he could not catch a drop. Then, yes! Success. A trickle! A deluge! An ecstasy! O happy end! Clunk! Clunk! Clunk! Clunk! Sssh, rattle, vrooomh, rattle, rattle, sssssh, nnnnnnnnnn. Stop. The dream turned to nightmare.

"No..! Who turned the water off? Please, please!"

James was in fever, tortured by the memory of all the water in his past. The water he had wasted while running taps. Gallons running unused down the sewers. The waste when overfilling the bath, water slopping over the sides, spilling on to the floor ... All the ridiculous opportunities he had wasted by failing to drink swimming pool water, rainwater. And worse, the chance he missed to drink the whole White Nile when he had traveled up the river from Cairo ... All the insane times he could have drunk sea water, dish water, toilet bowl water.

Totally insane.

But any water was better than no water to James at that moment. For the shower-head nightmare returned.

"No please, don't turn it off. Please, no!"

On and on and on went his nightmare. There was no rest from water as he tossed and turned and tried to escape. In his memory, tearing at his mind was an ice cool beer, a refreshing fruit juice, or a clear glass of sparkling cold water. Tearing, ripping him to shreds.

SUNDAY

Dawn.

The sky behind the mountains tinted red.

Weak but still capable of movement, James knew he was finished if he didn't start to walk. His feet in pain, he pulled himself to an upright position and began following the road that turned along the foot of a mountain.

"How much further" he thought. "No food. No water. Today's my last day."

The sun reared from behind the mountain. A ray bisected the road to cut James off from the way ahead. He gritted his teeth as the first impact of another torturous day commenced. The memory of his previous lessons was still fresh and raw.

The early morning shadows gone, his feet, his thirst, his hunger went beyond bounds he could never have dreamed of. The thought of reaching Lokichogio had become a pretentious myth, a deceiving lie. Such a lie had been his permit for entry into hell.

Yet, still he did not regret his actions. His escape into the desert had gone beyond reoccurring doubts. He accepted it all as a short cut to the doors of a better earthly Heaven than the one he had left behind with an impatient slam. Waiting in Kappoeta had been a nightmare.

James halted panting, sweating and too dry mouthed to speak to himself. He could taste blood coming up from his insides. His nosebleed had stopped. He felt nauseous and dizzy. He didn't know how much longer he could go on.

He picked a thorn bush and took shade. A half, another quarter, a full hour passed, he didn't move. Then slowly the thought of staying there longer brought on fears of death. With great effort he picked himself up, and staggered on, not knowing how far he'd walked or how far he still had to go.

Two more miles. Two searing, evil miles walked or not, it didn't seem to matter much. He kept going, until grabbed by an excruciating pain, he careered off the road disregardful of lacerating thorns, spearing cactus, slashing brushwood. Aimed like a guided missile after launch, he homed-in on the shade offered by a small tree. With increasing velocity, he tumbled, whistled down on target.

He lunged into a gaping crater, and entrenched, he groaned like a dying soldier, so thankful of the shelled out shade that now saved him from the deadly rays of the invincible sun.

Until evening he hardly moved, except for an occasional attempt to urinate. Weak-kneed, eyes closed, he sat on a long knotted bough springing from the base of a dying tree. He tried to excrete, but only succeeded in pissing into his unlaced boots. The heat soon dried his boots out, vague whiffs of smelly steam faintly visible. With his dreams of water in the past, thoughts of finishing the ordeal or being finished took over. Too late, it occurred to him that he could have drunk his urine. He started talking to himself.

"I guess I've got to walk. Christ, I'm much too weak."

He looked about and imagined he was back in London.

"Where is Kentish Town from here? Euston, Camden, Chalk Farm. Heh! You're on the wrong line. Got to walk, but I'm getting weaker. What are we doing on Tavistock Hill. Feathers Road at that. Number 20. Who lives there? Don't ask me. Ask the tenant. Maybe soon I can't walk. All these sulfates are supposed to help. I sometimes wonder. Got to walk, but half a weight of grass doesn't help the brain co-ordinate. Soon be there though."

James suddenly hauled himself to his feet.

"Linda! Do you hear me? I'm

getting weaker, do you hear?"

He had begun to walk again.

"I must walk but my load is too heavy. I'm too weak. Tell me how I can find my way to Royal College Street. Ah, may be, yes. If I left my bag. I see, yes that's it. Flat 11 in entrance 242. Yes I've got it. I could come back once I've made it. Yes, what's that, Linda? Walking would be easier. Yes."

He imagined the bushes were talking to him.

"Only what? Only twelve miles. Without a load and a bag of vegetables. Four hours. Brussels, cabbage, courgettes. Only four hours, then we'll make it. Yes. I hope I'm not too weak. What say you, woman in Kentish Town?"

James was beyond consciousness, yet something was pushing him on.

"I'm getting weaker, but I must try to stand. The flower seller perhaps some day will give me a five-penny discount. No, I'm much too weak. But I must. Yes I must. Got to stand, got to walk, only four hours, yes only four............ "

James left his pack under a bush as the sun dying, died. He shuffled to the road, tight mouthed, face a ghastly white, each future mile a call for rest, every half hour bring him to his knees. After the third mile, James collapsed and lay gazing up at the moon, big and glowing. He dozed off and awoke to find the moon moving across the sky. It was weird.

Suddenly, he felt the bursting desire to excrete.

"No! he cried, pulling down his pants.

In a crouch he waited for the onrush. But nothing happened.

"Wind."

He pulled his pants up again and lay back down to stare at the moon. He was too exhausted to move. The desire came again. He whipped down his pants, but the feeling died. He lay down again, no longer part of the world, and began to float beyond previous experience. Then feeling the urge to shit again, he crawled on his hands and knees, pulled down his shorts, and squeezed out the tiniest shit of his life on to the naked ground. Most of it was blood.

Death was knocking, and nearly gaining an answer.

Only James's semi-conscious was left aware. His fat had turned to flesh. He was a skeleton capable of nothing but thought for water. He had tried to alleviate his constipation and was incapable. Yet it had made him decide that he didn't want to spend the last dropping of his life by the side of that forsaken road. By God, no. He wished to live.

"Pick yourself up, cunt" he told himself. "You're not passing out of life with a measly trickle like that. One measly little slurpy shit oozing out from you? By Christ, no, you bastard. Get up! Go on, get up!"

He was up, and staggering. In his imagination he was back in the Boy's Brigade leading them round the drill hall, following the white lines.

"LEFT! RIGHT! LEFT! RIGHT! .... Company about......... Wheeeeel! Company......... One. Two. Three. Halt!"

Fuuuuummp!

James was back on the ground again, close to the end. He met with the hand of wooden death, an eerie shape by the moonlight. He lay watching his own hand shake the remains of the extended hand of a five-fingered dead wood branch. The Germans were all around in symphonies of Bach, Beethoven, dark serene triumphant death, peace and tranquility in the sight of life run dry. The pain was forgotten. He had been forced beyond to where his body tingled in an opium dream, his senses dulled by the sedation of pleasure. Rocks were no longer quartz or feldspar with iron inclusion, but cushions of the softest down. Each thorn had become the Indian nail bed of a meditating guru who felt no pain.

Yet the peace was so brief. The change came as he sought peace. Change as he sought peace, deep peace. Change. No, peace. Change! No! Change! No! There was no peace as the tormenting wind would not let him sleep. The joy of pain was turning into a world of waste and evil. It was driving him from his sheltered hollow to fight again, to battle and challenge.

"Don't accept your coming death brother" a voice said to him. "Risk it. A life-time's gamble is much better than a coffin of thorns and rocks and finding another layer of whitened bones upon the pile of all the past dust bitten heroes, who gave up the fight, threw in the will to carry on without using their every strength to keep from dying. Why accept death so soon. Thirty-seven is the golden age for death, and not before. Remember that. Don't give in. Twenty-two years old, dear James is far too young to flunk the class.

Death knocked again, but James was up and walking, staggering, crawling across a dried up riverbed. His legs did not finally give-in until he fell against the door of a shack and collapsed at the feet of two Kenyan policemen.

POSTSCRIPT

Since the time this story took place, Southern Sudan has became an independent state. There is now an official border post between Kenya and Southern Sudan at Nadapal, two kilometers north of Lokichogio, the spot where James had his 'symphony' visions.

ROBBIE MOFFAT

The author was born and schooled in Glasgow. He took a degree in English language and Literature at Newcastle University. He began writing when he was seventeen and has a had a career as a poet, novelist, playwright and screenwriter. He is best known for his feature film work in which he is also a director and producer.

His prose writing as been overshadowed by this. He wrote his first novel when he was twenty two and continued to write novels for the next twenty years. None of them were published.

The rediscovery of his prose work has lead to a recent spate of publications that has lead to a resurgence of interest in his prose work.